SPECULATIONS III

POETRY
FROM
THE WEIRD POETS SOCIETY

ISBN 978-1-7367114-2-2

MIND'S EYE

PUBLICATIONS ™

SPECULATIONS

III

POETRY FROM
THE WEIRD POETS SOCIETY

Welcome Reader

Welcome to this third *SPECULATIONS* anthology, offering a selection from some of the members of the Weird Poets Society Facebook group. We are a collection of Poets of the Speculative. Most of our poetic work is in the genres of the Weird, Horrific, Supernatural, Science Fictional, Fantastic, and across the spectrum of the various sub-genres of Adventure.

There are poets in this small tome who have but lately broken into these specialized market areas; there are some who have published many volumes and many individual poems—some who have been nominated or won some of the highest honors in speculative poetry.

Many of the writers represented herein are also members of either or both the Horror Writers Association and the Science Fiction & Fantasy Poetry Association. To be a member of the Weird Poets Society, one must have published speculative poetry (either individual poems or in chapbooks, collections, or anthologies) in any of the above mentioned genres or sub-genres.

You will find both formalist poets and practitioners of various modes of free verse. You will encounter a broad variety of themes and perspectives. This tome provides an excellent sampling of the work of several of our members.

Please peruse and enjoy our annual collaborative anthology, *SPECULATIONS III*, primarily containing published works from 2020, but also including some first-time appearances.

Frank Coffman, Editor
Moderator, Weird Poets Society Facebook Site
Elgin, Illinois
15 July 2021

TABLE OF CONTENTS

ILLUSTRATIONS

Manuel Arenas is a writer of verse and prose in the Gothic Horror tradition. His work has appeared in *Spectral Realms* and *Penumbra*, respectively, as well as various genre anthologies; including (most recently) *Knock Knock: Wyrd Folks* and *Wive's Tales* from Frisson Comics.

He currently resides in Phoenix, Arizona, where he pens his dark ditties sheltered behind heavy curtains, as he shuns the oppressive orb which glares down on him from the cloudless, dust-filled sky.

Hell-Flower

At Hecate's prompt, Hell-Flower blooms:
Ray florets open, awash in streams,
Of moonshine splayed athwart crumbling tombs,
Dappling headstones in argent beams.

Bathing in full moon luminescence,
Wafting in fetor of Hell-mouth breath,
Perfumed airs of graveyard putrescence,
The potpourri of decaying death.

Drawing sustenance from coffined ground.
Fecund, yet foul, beyond potter's field.
Stretching its roots in unhallowed mound,
Cornucopia of unclean yield.

Puce petals frame a floral death's head,
Smiling with teeth absorbed from the soil.
Gnawing morsels purloined from the dead,
Wriggling amidst defiled charnel spoil.

—Manuel Paul Arenas

Leigh Blackmore's horror fiction has appeared in over 60 magazine titles from *Avatar* to *Strange Detective Stories*. He has reviewed for journals including *Lovecraft Annual, Shoggoth, Skinned Alive* and *Dead Reckonings*. His critical essays appear in volumes including Szumskyj, Benjamin (ed.), *The Man Who Collected Psychos: Critical Essays on Robert Bloch*; Crawford, Gary W (ed.), *Ramsey Campbell: Critical Essays on the Modern Master of Horror*; and Olson, Danel (ed.), *21st Century Gothic* and elsewhere. New weird verse is forthcoming in *Penumbra, Spectral Realms* and other journals.

Ice-Demons

Upon tall peaks caliginous and cold
Where frost and snow perpetually lie
And gales blow hard where glaciers have rolled,
Strange shapes are glimpsed in motion up on high.

Occluded by the sheets of sleet and snow,
These dismal creatures, galling to discern.
Aphotic realms where chill winds always blow
Surround Them, as Their fierce eyes redly burn.

Abhorrent creatures formed from jagged ice –
The Wendigo, Their cousin. Mortals sleep;
Ice-demons flock, their victims to entice --
Demoniac destruction They will reap.

This night They wing, descending on the town
That spreads below, to make Their deadly raid
Against the folk who dwell there, flying down
To wreak Their icy vengeance - evil clade!

Foison enough to stab the hearts with ice
Of innocents who live their lives in peace --
Harvest of human souls to pay such price
As demons deem is owing, without cease.

Ice-demons strike! Their fiendish talons freeze
And sink into the warm flesh, heart and bone.
This sacrifice no godhead shall appease!
They fly, returning to harsh worlds of stone.

—Leigh Blackmore

--first appeared in *Woolongong* (July and Aug 2020)

"Menace" for "Ice Demons" by David M. Hoenig

Lamia

The lapidary lamia's lifetime .
Is spent a-crouch in lair of wet, black caves.
She curls her tail about her in the slime –
Seductress, harlot – her rough skin she laves.

Hetaira of the sovereign night, she waits
With horrent hairs upon her serpent tail --
A filthy glutton, made so by the Fates --
Enchantress, witch, Zeus-cursed one --white and pale,

Wide eyes unclosing, face twisted awry.
This odalisque of horror lures a child
Within her reach. Its piteous dying cry
Rings out, its life by succubus defiled.

This vampire daemon, almondine of eye,
Malevolent dark haunter of the night,
Bides awful time. Libyan Queen descry --
All humans perish here beneath her sight.

—Leigh Blackmore

first appeared in *Wollongong* (14 June , 8 Aug, 28 Aug 2020)

Bruce Boston lives in Ocala, Florida, once known as the City of Trees, with his wife, writer-artist Marge Simon, and the ghosts of two cats.

His poems and stories have appeared in hundreds of publications, most visibly in *Analog, Asimov's, Amazing Stories, Weird Tales, New Myths, Strange Horizons, The Pedestal Magazine, Realms of Fantasy, Daily Science Fiction, Year's Best Fantasy and Horror,* and the *Nebula Awards Showcase,* and received numerous awards, most notably the Bram Stoker Award, a Pushcart Prize, the Asimov's Readers Award, and the Rhysling and Grandmaster Awards of the Science Fiction & Fantasy Poetry Association.

His latest poetry collection, *Artifacts,* an Elgin Award Finalist, is available from Amazon and other online booksellers. http://bruceboston.com/

Devilish Incarnations

Bored with forging evil on an
hourly basis, the Devil decided
to retire to Palm Beach with
a covey of chosen concubines
who had pleasured his lust
through the millennial ages.

Now he indulges his needs,
both carnal and gustatory
on an hourly basis, downing
flagons of nectar, absinthe,
honey and nepenthe, sating
his hunger with immense
quantities of meals sublime,
indulging in prolonged priapic
encounters in the afternoons,
followed by glorious naps
rich in holocaustic dreams.

In the evenings the Devil
watches films old and new
on a full-scale screen
in the Grand Orpheum
of his private theater.

Some of his favorites:
Tod Browning's *Freaks*,
Joseph Mengele's lost
reels of the experiments
at Auschwitz, and the
compiled slow motion
footage of suicide
bombers detonating
in the crowded streets
and markets of Israel,
Pakistan, Iraq, Kuwait.

No need to worry about
the Devil's retirement.
His minions and their

many minions in turn,
their heirs everlasting
though the horrors of
the ages, are dedicated
to carry on all of his
fiendish endeavors that
prey upon the human spirit.

Just as they did before his
Incarnate Majesty claimed
the throne by trying on
his flaming scarlet skin.

The blades of sin may
be a little less sharp,
turn a little more slowly,
yet the cuts they leave
will be just as deep.

Now his minions wait
until some other worthy
savior arises to Father and
embody the Grand Tradition.

Perhaps the next incarnation
of his Maculate Majesty will
try on a skin that glows like
the rods of a nuclear reactor
ready to incandesce
in sacred conflagration.
Or he may opt for the most
common incarnation of all,
one human skin after another,
even many at the same time,
dying and being reborn,
over and over again with
kitbags full of hate and evil.

—Bruce Boston
first appeared in the Science Fiction & Fantasy Poetry Association journal,
Star*Line, Jan-Feb, 2020
Third Place winner in Long Poem category for the 2021 Rhysling Award

"Stray Grimoire" for "Devilish Incarnations" by David M. Hoenig

G. O. Clark's writing has been published in Asimov's, Analog, Space & Time, Midnight Under The Big Top, Daily SF, HWA Poetry Showcase VII and many other publications over the last 30 years. He's the author of 15 poetry collections, the most recent, "Easy Travel To The Stars", 2020.

His second fiction collection, "Twist & Turns", came out in 2016. He won the Asimov's Readers Award for poetry in 2001, and was Stoker Award finalist in 2011.

He's retired, and lives in Davis, CA.
http://goclarkpoet.weebly.com

Leisureville

One doesn't walk
around here after dark,
aware of the pulse beats of beasts
unseen lurking in the bushes,
tree branches overhead notched
by the claws of deadly raptors,
their reptile brains primed for
carrion slaughter.

One stays home,
doors and windows locked,
avoiding the garrulous gnomes,
pale plaster angels with broken
wings, hungry Halloween skulls,
and the blood stained shovels, rakes,
hoes, tomato trellis traps and
other garden club tools of torture,
waiting in the shadows of tool sheds
to prune and pulverize.

One doesn't linger
outside the darkened windows
of these tomb-like mobile homes
that line the circular streets and
pathways, divorced from the world
at large, midnight marking the time
of open season upon insomniacs out for
a moonlit stroll; trigger happy, wary seniors
defending their final leases on life against
old nightmares childhood born;
never forgotten.

—G. O. Clark
first appeared in *HWA Poetry Showcase, Vol. VII, 2020.*

Post-Obit Cautionary Tale

We were told
not to go into the cave,
parents strictly forbidding us,
signs warning beware.

Monsters were said to
dwell within its cold, damp walls;
maleficent, blood craving, and
patient as Death.

Double dares are
binding when you're young and
foolish; consequences
always be damned.

On that rainy Fall night,
flashlights clutched in trembling
hands, bravado urging us forward,
the cave bid us welcome.

Back in town, the monthly
school board meeting droned on,
and beer taps at the local
bar flowed freely.

Our screams were
lost in the night, the smell
of shredded, young flesh masked
by the pungent woods.

Empty beds and
school desks bore witness
next morning; new fears triggered,
bad memories refreshed.

—G. O. Clark

first appeared in *Tales From the Moonlight Path, July 2020*.

Frank Coffman is a retired professor of college English, Creative Writing, and Journalism. He has published speculative poetry and fiction in a variety of magazines and anthologies. His poetic magnum opus, *The Coven's Hornbook & Other Poems* (2019) has been followed by his rendition into English Verse of 327 quatrains of *Khayyám's Rubáiyát* (2019). A second large collection of poetry, *Black Flames & Gleaming Shadows* was published in 2020.

A traditional formalist in his poetic work, he is especially interested in exploring and experimenting with the patterns of verse found across the world's cultures and ethnicities and across time from ancient to modern. His special love of and interest in the sonnet has led to invention of several cross-cultural meldings of various traditions with the 14-line restriction of the sonnet form.

His third poetry collection, *Eclipse of the Moon*, was published in May 2021. A collection of seven of his occult detective stories, *Three Against the Dark*, will be published in late 2021, and a collection of weird and supernatural short stories, *Summa Terrorem: Tales of Horror and the Supernatural*, is projected for 2022.

A member of the Horror Writers Association and the Science Fiction & Fantasy Poetry Association. He established and moderates the *Weird Poets Society* Facebook group. See his Writer's Blog at: https://www.frankcoffman-wordsmith.com

The Pathways of R'lyeh

(an Irregular Megasonnet)

Deep-diving the Pacific at the spot
That's furthest off from any mass of land,*
The Bathyship was doing wondrous work.
The depths were lighted, and the sonar scanned
Those black-dark waters where strange creatures lurk.

We found the place that reason says cannot
Be real! And yet—a nightmare of the deep
Lies there among the drifting ooze and weeds.
We dared to enter through a cyclopean gate
Of monstrous stones in shapes I can't relate!
A city's there! In weird and age-old sleep!
But to describe it?! No human tongue succeeds.

Yes! We had found R'lyeh—that city of myth!
At least we thought those horrid tales untrue—
Mere ramblings to frighten, fables of the sea!

We dared to cruise down one strange avenue,
The lines of which confound geometry.
The city center loomed, green gloom like Death
Hung all about. Then, suddenly, we knew!
Dreaming—though Dead! We fled! We had to flee
From those depths! For we saw what lies beneath!

*Point Nemo, The "Pole of Inacessibility" This remote oceanic location is
located at coordinates 48°52.6' S 123°23.6' W, about 2,688 kilometers from the
nearest land—Ducie Island, part of the Pitcairn Islands, to the north; Motu
Nui, one of the Easter Islands, to the northeast; and Maher Island, part of
Antarctica, to the south.

—Frank Coffman

first appeared in *Black Flames & Gleaming Shadows*, Bold Venture Press, 2020

Warnings to the Curious

"The hotel room was adequate, pleasant enough.
Weary as I was, any haven would suffice.
Without, the wind howled wildly, cold as ice.
A sleet- and hail-filled time, the journey rough
From Salem out to Arkham in my car.
And I could barely see the road before me!
I can't recall a night so fierce and stormy;
It took three grueling hours, though not that far.

"Upon the nightstand, close beside the bed,
There lay a book—'A Bible,' I thought at first—
'But this one's odd?' Not covered black or red
Like most of them. And it was in the worst
Condition I had ever seen. It's pages
Were dark-discolored and its cover worn:
A dingy yellow—a most sickly hue!
Strangely, I felt uneasy just to view
The thing. And, stranger still, no words were born
Upon the cover. So, I looked inside.

"I should have stopped when I read that old scrawl
Upon the flyleaf's formerly blank face:
'By all that's Holy, don't read beyond this place!
Friend, if you value your sanity and all
Or any joys you've known ere reading this,
Put this tome down or thrown it in the fire!—
Destroy it! Though that is my great desire,
Having read—I can't!—and now there is no bliss,
No comfort for me now, no going back
To the life I had before I read this book.
For that old, normal world I have forsook.
Now I am doomed—and all my vistas black!'

"Somehow, despite this weird and warning note,
I felt myself compelled to turn the leaf
To see if that was all the scribbler wrote—
Then saw the title page. This tome of grief
Was one I'd heard of many years ago.

15

'The stuff of legend;' I had always thought,
'A myth to frighten.' So, I'd never sought
To find it, let alone to seek to know
What lay within those pages steeped in lore.
But now I held a copy in my hands.
I thought, 'What harm to just explore
The first few pages?'

                          "No one understands
The pull that awful book has on one's mind
Until they have the misfortune, as I did,
To read those horrid words that should be hid
In the darkest depths of Hell that one could find!

"So, stranger, heed you well these words of warning:
Reading The King in Yellow dooms your soul!
Your life becomes a night that knows no morning,
No solace as your few scant seasons roll
On toward those horrors that words cannot define.
For I have seen the King in yellow tatters,
Carcosa, and the realms where reason shatters,
The Old Ones terrible, The Yellow Sign!

"What of my mind remains tells me I should
Destroy this book—in the name of all that's Good
And Holy. And I'd destroy it—if I could!
I leave that task to you. Do not read on!
Resist that urge. And learn to love the dawn!"
* * *

"How curious," he thought, "clearly two different hands?"
The book in his hotel room's bedside drawer
Was one that he had heard of oft before.
'By all that's Holy…' and 'No one understands…'
   He'd been hired as Miskatonic's latest sage.
   "What harm?" he thought,…

                          then turned another page.

—Frank Coffman

first appeared in *Black Flames & Gleaming Shadows*, Bold Venture Press, 2020

"The Book" for "Warnings to the Curious" by David M. Hoenig

The Wheel of the Year

(a sequence in the Old Irish meter of Rannaighheacht Mhor)

YULE

Old Year dies with Darkest Night.
Dim at Dawn the ghost light lies;
Fleet flies day in grim grey dight;
The Sun through Noon's Low height hies.

Time of Yule has come again,
When both End and Renewal
Rule. The New Year must begin.
But, in Winter, Earth cries cruel.

Garner we the golden grain.
Hunger's bane, bone-biting cold,
Age-old ills, starvation's pain
Wanes if stock are in full fold.

Some led to slaughter—for feast;
All beasts cannot be well fed
In fair folks' stead. They are least;
Druid priest rules they be bled.

Twelve days, mirth filled, we celebrate.
The Great Wheel turns, New Year's birth
Will break dread dearth—Old Year's fate—
Soon or late give green to Earth.

Twelve long nights, by great log's blaze,
We praise, through feasting and song,
The Great Mother's strong wild ways.
Days lengthen; cruel Winter's wrong

Must die. And on the Twelfth Night
Great bonfires alight. Flames fly
High toward the heavens. That bright
Light helps the day's dark deny.

Bold Dark Time, both Last and First,
Worst in dreadful snow and cold,

For untold ages blessed, cursed,
We nurse the New, oust our Old.

IMBOLC
Imbolc. Fair Earth is fecund,
New seeds beckoned toward birth.
Dearth Days' ending is reckoned,
This second quarter, make mirth.

Waters flowing deep have found
Earthbound Life. Rain and snowing
Are knowing in planted mound
Life in the dark ground growing.

Go we to the sacred well.
Druid's tell the milk should flow,
Great Mother knows that this spell,
libation will swell, green grow

The shoots as the sweet Spring nears.
Untold years, meet we to meet,
Defeat Winter, conquer fears.
Feasting cheers and fires great greet

World's warming. Lambings will begin.
In Imbolc's weather a charm,
If warm—and Sun wears a grin—
Cailleach's bin she fills; hard harm.

She wakes, gathers her firewood.
Then should all folk, for their sake,
Make ready for more cold. But good
If Sky wears Hood. Winter will break.

Winter's yolk's end we foresee
And so do all our free folk
Icy cloak melts. Gather we
'Round the sacred oak. Imbolc.

OSTARA

Ostara opens the door
for new life. Now Spring begins.
Day, dark Night of equal length
give strength. O season bold, bright!

Balance between Life and Death!
Breath of the Earth—God of Green
marries Mother Earth again!
When the trickster hare hurries

once more through bramble and brush,
lush and wet, the land renews.
Nurtured in nests—strange eggs laid.
Eostre made a magic change:

found a bird with broken wing—
she saved the thing with spoken
spell, sorcery set to guard
with words. Now all stories tell

how it became an odd hare!
There, in rabbit nest, the god
one true bird trait left displayed:
eggs are laid—now the hare's fate!

In field, fold, and forest wan
(Pan of eld, as tale is told)
The Horned God pipes in the green.
Broadly seen—Spring's beauties born.

Dawn Sun God yolk, days lengthen
White Goddess, strengthens the folk.
Full moon will see a great feast!
Ostara in East—Spring soon.

BELTANE

Sweet day of Beltane is born!
Both kine and corn in array

are blessed! May Earth's green cloak worn
adorn now new soft Spring's sway!

In keeping with our old ways,
As Sun soars, slays Winter's sleep,
flames leap! Druid fires ablaze
in this phase, with dwimmer deep

and weird Wizard words of praise.
We bring the cattle. We herd
them betwixt two balefire's blaze.
Thus Earth's blessings are conferred.

Bedight by yellow flowers,
Pure powers of Earth's rebirth swell.
Now knell sounds of Winter's hours.
Fire devours cold. We quell

the entrance of Aos Si;
we make offerings and dance,
prance over embers, and we
with glee bake bannocks, enhance

Protection of flock and field,
wold and weald. So crops will grow
we know the bannock bits wield
power, yield blessings—so we throw

some to the Si to guard sheep,
keep safe our kine, and to ward
fox, wolf from our yards. The Deep
of Dearth is done. Sleeping hard

for long, the loved Earth awakes,
shaken from rest with strong song.
Along World's Rim warm dawn breaks,
Streams fill lakes, birds join the throng.

LITHA

Litha! Leaping sun flies high!
Nigh the longest day we praise,
raise our chants, the Dark defy,
glorify the Long Day's rays.
On High Hills the Great Fires rise.
Dark's demise comes with the dawn.
Gone Earth's Deathtime. Summer skies
smile as flies Sol's fire disk, drawn

by the bright Steeds of the Day;
Songs pray to the Lord of Light.
Bright green, Earth's Mother holds sway.
At bay the might of nether Night.

Midsummer! Smoke rises, brings
Kings' clash! The Holly and Oak
convoke both Night and Light. Things
balance! But Dark Wings invoke

drear dwindling of each next day,
vexed, they march toward Yule of year.
But cheer we now—no dismay
allays our Sun-blessed play here.

LUGNASADH

First fruits of Old Earth we glean!
Earth's green has now turned to gold!
In field and in fold are seen
the scenes of a tale retold.

Once again the god has won;
Strong Sun and the ample rain
and Lugh's mighty strain have done
to death Blight—the harvest's bane.

We bake bread, offer a bull;
A full feast, merry we make.
Holy Lake and Holy Well
shall we travel to this week.

Athletic contests we hold.
From of old the games are set,
Met from wide and far, the bold
over wold race horses yet,
still stick-fight, throw weights around.
Matches found as maid meets beau.
All know Life's riches abound
as sounds of our revels grow.

The three-faced god do we praise;
raise altars to Lugh, and grace
those places with grain. Sun's rays
warm, but the shadows trace,

in longer lines on the grass,
lingering but lessening song.
The thronging of birds yet bless
Day's Reign—but each day less long.

MABON
Day and dark are twins again,
when the Divine Son holds sway.
We pray to Mabon and Matron.
Harvest begins; feast and play

mark Autumn's opening, blessed
with zest for Life. And we sing,
praising the Horned God's quest—
the Test each long year to bring

plentiful the Harvest Home,
roam forest and fold. For he
frees—though briefly—Winter's gloom—
though looms the yearly Death he'll see.

Thanks all give, bounty sharing,
faring into Earth's Great Fall.
Year End's pall, stalled by caring,
dare not mar Life's joyous call.

SAMHAIN

Samhain begins. Blessed Sun dies
down skies turned blood. So now,
though years Bright Half fleetly flies,
hies, as once more it must go,
glow the Great Fires, druids round,
sound strong prayers, to abate
fell Fate to which Earth is bound.
Found by fey fiends. Now is The Gate,

by feared Lord of Death flung wide,
denied to damned wights through the year,
they near us now, this eventide,
ride abroad to hound us here.

Don we now grim mask and guise,
pray cries will ward off fiendish foes.
Bright go embers to black skies,
rise and fade as Earth's warmth goes.

Great Fires light the way for friends.
Though ends the Year's bright half this night,
we pray it frightens, trust it sends
Evil to wend home at its sight.

Feasting, we save special places
for faces we shall no more see.
Though dead they be, some traces
may grace our live family.

Harvest store must all be home.
Roam the grazing stock no more;
gore of slaughter lies on loam—
some saved, to breed as before.

Bones bare from slaughter and feast
are cast into the central fire—
where Druids, as through ages past
have blessed those the gods require.

Year's Bright Half must be reborn—
Horned God, Great Mother. So, this night,
rite of human blood is borne.
And Torn Veil must be mended right.

—Frank Coffman

first appeared in *Black Flames & Gleaming Shadows*, Bold Venture Press, 2020

NOTES ON FORMS

The Megasonnet
I've invented forms of what I call the "Megasonnet." Essentially, it is an expansion of well-known sonnet forms into 21 line forms.

The "English Megasonnet" expands the quatrains plus couplet structure of the Shakespearean abab cdcd efef gg into three hexains and a tercet: abcabc defdef ghighi jjj (or jxj where x is any of the three rhymes of the last hexain: jgj, jhj, or jij). Hence 21 lines.

The "Italian Megasonnet" expands the octave and sestet of the Petrarchan abbaabba || cdcdcd or cdecde into a "duodecave/duodecade" and a "nontet/ nonastich": abccbaabccba || defdefdef. Hence 21 lines.

"The Pathways of R'yleh" is an "irregular" Megasonnet in its division and its random rhyme pattern. Still 21 lines.

"Warnings to the Curious" is a Nonce Form

Rannaighheacht Mhor
(pron. Ron-á-yach Voor "Great Versification")
"The Wheel of the Year" is an English approximation of this measure
- 7-syllable quatrains
- rhymed abab
- two words in each line must alliterate
- the end words must cross rhyme in each couplet
- the last word of line four alliterates with the previous word
- uses dúnadh ("conclusion") where the poem ends with the same phoneme, syllable, word, or phrase as it began. NOTE: This and other strict parameters have not followed in all of these segments.

Scott J. Couturier is a poet & prose writer of the Weird, grotesque, liminal, & darkly fantastic. His work has appeared in numerous venues, including *The Audient Void, Spectral Realms, Eye To The Telescope, The Dark Corner Zine, Space and Time Magazine, & Weirdbook.*

Currently he works as a copy & content editor for Mission Point Press, living an obscure reverie with his partner/live-in editor & two cats.

The Idiot God

The Idiot God, struck mad with machinations,
dumbed by the din of Time winding down.
Throne coated in crabbed arcane notations,
fiery brow fraught, lips fixed in marmoreal frown.

Above swirl storm-clouds of psychoses' creation,
lightning lancing thunderless to deadened thews.
Below, cosmoses of Creator's ideation
learn the stupefied silence of their sire to rue.

Opaline eyes fixed on the void beyond void,
babbling dumb words to worlds inchoate, eager
to encompass any demiurgic urge devoid
of dotard's pathos: pining for Archimedes' lever!

But no sensible will this ill deity portends:
only Eternity of barren, sickly stupor,
endless beginnings without any ends.
The stars weep tears of flame at Divine torpor.

—Scott J. Couturier

first appeared in *Cosmic Horror Monthly issue #1*

The Crimson Knight

A knight in crimson armor stands
upon a crimson shore:
waves break at her iron-beaked feet,
swells of godly gore.
She had come to taste of this red sea
& thus immortal become:
Yet now, Death seems more a friend
than foe to begrudge a sum.
She has come to pity the Gods for their
excesses & their might –
She has seen the vales of endless wrack,
the weals of Promethean night.
She has slain a thousand, thousand men,
enfeebled countless more,
all to reach these ichor-imbued sands,
this rank & crimson shore.
She stares, and is appalled by crawling
things that flop & moan:
her gorge rises as the seaside froths
with semi-sentient foam.
Her sword, chipped & stained to jet
by blood of lover, friend, & foe
now is driven deep into her heart –
a barb of bitterest woe.
Out amid those erubescent waves
Titans up-stir, wail & cry:
That she should come so far to attain
what all inherit – that is, to die.

—Scott J. Couturier

first appeared in *Spectral Realms issue #12*

Harris Coverley has speculative verse published and forthcoming in *Star*Line, Polu Texni, Spectral Realms, Scifaikuest, View From Atlantis, Horror Sleaze Trash, Schlock! Webzine, and Lovecraftiana,* as well as more mundane (but still pretty damn good) fare in *New Reader Magazine, Better Than Starbucks, Corvus Review, Ariel Chart, Abandoned Library Press, Artifact Nouveau, Mad Swirl, Scarlet Leaf Review, Ordinary Madness,* and *Yellow Mama,* amongst many others.

A member of the Weird Poets Society since 2018, he is also a fictionist, with short stories published and forthcoming in *Curiosities, Hypnos, The Periodical, Forlorn, Frost Zone Zine,* and *Horla.*

He lives in Manchester, England, where he quasi-reluctantly patterns his life after that of Ignatius J. Reilly and James Shelley of the 1980s ITV sitcom *Shelley.*

Nub

She came in
through the front door
and hung the
universe on a hook
on the wall.

I then cried
tears of gold
that she baked
into biscuits.

We then sat
and watched
TV.

Love is so often
like ice cream
melting in
your mouth.

I could cry
some more,
but no gold
these days.

Just salt tears.

—Harris Coverley

first appeared in *The Oddville Press, Winter 2020*

Allegrons

a loose melody
played on Einstein's violin
in relative time

—Harris Coverley

first appeared in *Utopia Science Fiction, Vol. 1, Issue 06, June 2020*

Home Invasion of the Complete Bastard from Outer Space: A Yuletide Verse

For John Cooper Clarke

Got an alien for Christmas—what a to-do!
Put a festive jumper on him and he screamed "Screw you!"
He tore it right off and ran up the wall
Then he swung from the light and kneed me in the balls

Got an alien for Christmas—rather me dad hadn't bothered
The purple git drank all the Baileys and now he's buggered
He sicked acid in the front room and it burnt to the cellar
Now he's on the bathroom floor singing Paul Weller

Got an alien for Christmas—and he made a play for the girlfriend!
Ten hands is a lotta hands—she thought it'd never end!
He got real narked and puked up some more
Now he's crying face down on the kitchen floor

Got an alien for Christmas—and he's a pain in the arse
He sits in dad's armchair and says we've no class
He says this mind over his tenth can of brew
And then he turns to his left and his guts he does spew

Got an alien for Christmas—and he's pissed off next door
Threw a brick through his window and called his mother a whore
It took a hell of a lot to hold the raging guy back
As that monster flipped him off and swilled more cognac

Got an alien for Christmas—and he's fucked things right up
All he does is complain and all the booze he does sup
I think it might be time for this twat to phone home
Or else to green-blooded murder will someone be prone

Got an alien for Christmas—and the bastard has gone
We registered our close encounter—the "kind"? Minus one.

—Harris Coverley

first appeared in *View From Atlantis, Issue 21 (December 2020)*

Margaret (Margi) CURTIS (b. 1957) (Master of Creative Arts, Grad. Dip. *Transpersonal Breathwork*), witch, writer, artist, healer and activist, lives in Wollongong, NSW, Australia with her family and a black cat. Published in magazines and anthologies, in print and online, including *Midnight Echo* and *Spectral Realms*, she is the author of four collections of poetry including V*oice of the Goddess and other poems* (1991). Margi is currently offering a two-year Training in Priestessing the Revolution.

Beltane

"This is the time when sweet desire weds wild delight. The Maiden of Spring and the Lord of the Waxing Year meet in the greening fields and rejoice together under the warm sun. The shaft of life is twined in a spiral web and all of nature is renewed. We meet in the time of flowering, to dance the dance of life."

— Starhawk, *The Spiral Dance.*

When limbs of trees display fresh leafy dress
And tendrils new emerge from sidewalk cracks,
When sunshine softens winter's cold caress
And loosens our stiff shoulders, warms our backs,
I wander out in search of alleys dark
And city streets that take me far from home,
Until I chance upon that secret park
Where, at this time of year, the strangers come.

I find the gathered troupe, it seems by chance.
A Maypole standing, proud and well erect
Already marks the clearing for their dance,
With multi-coloured ribbons all bedecked,
The folk in costume here to celebrate
Some ancient rite of spring, once thought obscene.
I hesitate, while fear grips tight my heart,
I sense that I once dreamed these ways unseen
(And in this rite, I play some hidden part.)

Though I do not recall the lilt I hear
That trips so lightly from the drummer's hand
I find that I am drawn, despite my fear,
To join that masked, mysterious painted band.
We weave our ribbons slowly to and fro;
Two circles, face to face step in and out.
We bring the sky above to earth below
And faster still and faster, turn-about.

Time drops away as if the world is rent.
My breath comes ragged, catching in my chest
Before my ribbon's length at last is spent.

Into a heap I fall with all the rest
Of heaving bodies. Laughter and release
Descend around me. Someone clasps my hand.
I hear a panting whisper: "Choose me, please?"
I hear myself reply: "At your command!"

And in the twilight now I follow them
Between the cooling green of fern-fronds spun
With light and shade. We love as if become
The last on earth beneath a setting sun.
As in the fairytales of old they leave
Before I know their name, or offer mine;
Before the cock has crowed, before the breeze
Of dawn forewarns us of the night's decline.

I wander out again into a world
Renewed in ways familiar and strange.
I wonder at the parkland where unfurled
The rapture of a fateful welcome change.
No sign remains of revels that were here,
And though I find at last directions home,
That mystic pulse still whispers in my ear:
"My love, take heart, for we are not alone!"

—Margi Curtis

Don Gillette has been writing fiction, non-fiction, and poetry since Santa brought him one of the original "Tom Thumb" typewriters for his 6th birthday. He's published 5 novels, 4 poetry collections, and hundreds of short stories, reviews, newspaper, and magazine articles.

Don is currently at work on a novel, *Dark Voices*, and just completed editing a "group novel," *He Has Stayed Too Long*, with each of the 30 chapters written by a different author. Both books will be available in 2021.

You can follow Don on twitter @dongillette and on his website, dongillette.com.

Lady Lace

Can you force yourself to dream?
Can rivers freeze and skies erupt as you decree?
Do phantoms shriek from corners dark,
Impaling you on madness?
By which I mean can you decide?

Are you are the god of destiny,
Creator of the dark?
And is it wrong to cry so brightly
Diamonds crease your cheeks?
By which I mean do you exist?

Faceless, formless, through the night,
Creeping softly on their bellies,
Trapped inside deep, hollow loss
Lie glimpses of light, denying her hands.

Can you remember the Queen?
Do you hear her in the night?
Are her words scarce as the dawn is gone
On the sides of day?

—Don Gillette

The Sentinel's Samba

She dances the dance of the dead
On rainy evenings in palest moonlight
With dust scattering her flaying arms
And dirt rising in precious clouds
Around her sweaty legs.

The dirt takes on substance,
Finds its way upwards,
Rests on the glistening wet of her body.

She likes it that way
With its solid under solid,
Takes note of her steps as she picks up tempo
Beats the air, sends insects to the crowd,
Gains strength from the moon,
Gives it all for nothing.
We help keep her pace
Until midnight.

The dirt takes no notice of the next
As she turns and sways,
Tossing the strands of her skirt,
Pouting her lips at the sky
In an ecstasy inhuman.

—Don Gillette

Currently in her second-term as Poet Laureate of New Bedford, Massachusetts, author and playwright **Patricia Gomes** is the former editor of *Adagio Verse Quarterly,* and has been published in numerous literary journals and anthologies.

A 2018 and 2008 *Pushcart Prize* nominee, Gomes is the author of four chapbooks. Ms. Gomes recent publications include *Tidings, Star*Line, Muddy River Review, Rituals,* and *Apex and Abyss.*

Ms. Gomes is the co-founder of the GNB Writers Block as well a member of the Science Fiction & Fantasy Poetry Association, New England Horror Writers, the Horror Writers Association, and Massachusetts Poetry Society.

She writes — she is writing now — she will continue to write until she drops dead at her keyboard.

Tree Limbs Block the Road

These children of Slaughter
wander unsupervised,
over raw and barren landscapes
to plan treasons and red treachery
in icy caverns
that offer no warmth
to calm their evil proclivities.
No guilt, for what do they know but the soundless White?
Hairless demons with whirring brains,
their elongated teeth impale hope,
invite suicide.
Tendrils slither beneath the snow; close your heart, say your
prayers.
You'll hear them—do not be fooled by their childlike stature—
you'll hear them
slide around your doorframes, hissing
lewd and nauseating suggestions, licking your fear
from their bloodless lips.
Do not listen. They leave no footprints
and we've nothing:
no tool
no weapon

no remedy
nothing

to protect ourselves
from Winter Madness.

—Patricia Gomes

from *Wicked Women: An Anthology of New England Writers*
Wicked Women © 2020 The New England Horror Writers
Rhysling Award Nominees - The Anthology
Science Fiction & Fantasy Poetry Association © 2021

The Short Life of a Male Mantis

I had a poem
brewing
to honor the silent turn of the seasons,
or maybe the formation of designer ice cubes,
or possibly the beheading of a sated male mantis,
or, or, or ….
I don't remember, but it was something
along those lines.
I had a poem
brewing,

but I lost it

during the pandemic.
In the beginning, when blizzards were still conceivable
and bottles of rubbing alcohol steadfastly lined the shelves
at pharmacies like transparent alien soldiers in uniform.
Uncertainty hid it from me,   then
unease masked it,   until
panic enveloped it,
sealing it away in a wicker basket
meant for offerings.
I knew I'd never find it again.

Trapped—we two—the poet and the poem.
In quarantine, cornered
in a house where the windows rattle
and no one comes to visit.
Round and round we go, playing hide-n-seek
through endless political tirades and medical updates.
After the 11:00 PM news,
we whisper
seductive secrets to each other,   but still
it refuses to expose itself
to possible contamination.

—Patricia Gomes
Second Place Winner / Poets Choice Awards
Massachusetts State Poetry Society
Bay State Echo © 2020

David M. Hoenig is a multiclass surgeon/writer with the "time management" feat. He's had stories published with *Grim Dark Magazine, Flame Tree Publishing, Cast of Wonders*, and others. He has published a novel-told-through-surreal-verse-and-art with Oscillate Wildly Press, called *Queen To His King*.

He is editing his first novel (sci fi), at somewhat slower than the speed of light. He's also a soul-gem carrying member of the Horror Writers Association.

Social Butterfly Effect

Easy smiles, the new handshake,
repartee, the biz card give/take.
My clothes know who you are today;
algorithms in liquid crystal display
read kinesthesia, pitch and tones,
within my electrogenous zones.
Your data, contained by no condom,
splashes my blue dress like Kingdom
Come on, already! Got sensors for reasons:
don't remember birthdays, seasons,
dates, times, names, or faces,
if we met in the usual places,
virtual or pheromonal. Smart clothing's the real deal;
memory costs too much, but tech won't make you feel.

—David M. Hoenig

He Walks in Darkness

Beats the bright heart at the center;
tinkling goblets and laughter,
humming harps and conversation,
pattering dance steps and wit.

Light informs it all:
understanding, opportunity, unity.

But far and away, the light is eaten
by voracious, primal night.
Atavistic terrors lurk unseen,
gauging, always, weakness to exploit.

He walks in darkness,
for it is there that the vigil is called.

Malevolence stalks, just out of sight,
intent on feasting
the rich, vulnerable lifeblood
which churns so preciously.

The sentry hears the heart beating,
though not always the predator.

Yet there the dusk warrior marches,
in harm's way, undaunted,
the center he can hear so distantly
is not where he belongs.

His life on his own terms,
because he chooses to walk in darkness.

—David M. Hoenig

Geoffrey A. Landis is a science fiction writer and a scientist, as well as a poet. Recently he has spent a lot of his time working on the details of a mission to Neptune's moon Triton, and thinking about cities on Venus.

He is married to fellow poet and science fiction writer Mary Turzillo, and lives in Ohio, which has quite decent weather for 8 months of the year. His favorite dinosaur is pterodactyl, which technically isn't even a dinosaur at all.

Snow White and the Seven Deadly Sins

The fairy tale tells it wrong:
when she escaped the evil queen,
that pure and innocent virgin
wandered through the forest lost
until, weary,
exhausted of all hope,
she stumbled across the cave
of the Seven Sins.

Snow White became the servant
of the Seven Sins
(dwarven, indeed, in moral compass,
but deadly giant in power among mortals)
and learned from them
their ways,
and learned from them
their power.

With her power,
inflamed with envy
engorged with lust
inflated with pride
sharp with wrath
greedy and gluttonous for her kingdom:
what need had such as she
for a prince?

Oh, yes,
luminous in all her deadly glory,
throbbing with her new-forged power,
glowing with her white-hot wrath –
she had every intent of returning to her kingdom
except that,
suffused and satiated with the seventh of the sins,
Sloth,
she fell asleep.

Oh, prince,
will you be the one?
Will you wake her?

—Geoffrey A. Landis
first appeared in *Space & Time*, May 2020

A World of Ghosts

A ghost is just a memory made thick:
a chill in the air, a flicker in the night.
Ghosts are regrets that linger in silence,
a footstep half heard, movement just out of sight.

We live in a world of myriad ghosts,
of all those before us, all that have gone since;
the good and the bad, their lives forgotten,
the echo of footsteps, erased by the winds.

The dead all about us outnumber the living,
their voices unspeaking, their blood smoke in their veins.
Their loves and their hatreds, their passion still lingers,
their pride and their fury and their hope and their pain.

Their cries are not silent just because we don't hear them,
the past never dies, is not gone, does not fade;
the crystalline amber of frozen eternity,
innumerable, invisible, intangible, unchanged.

So, say a prayer for those who surround you
invisible, immortal, immanent, unseen.
Light them a candle to hold back the darkness,
what is and what could be, what was and has been.

—Geoffrey A. Landis

first appeared in *Siren's Call, 52, Winter 2020*

The Forest, in the Full of the Moon

The forest is different in the night.
In the moonlight, the forest belongs
to the court of the goblin king.

Listen: strain your ears.
Do you hear the faint strands
of faerie horns blowing far away?

In the goblin market,
kobolds and hobgoblins haggle,
paying with shards of moonlight.

Only the silence of owl's wings,
only the hush of indrawn breath.
The forest dark with dappled shadows.

Sylphs splash in silver puddles,
and between the folds of the crystalline night
dark eyed fauns pause to watch.

You might bargain for your heart's desire,
or barter your heart for a handful of moonbeams.
Or do your mortal eyes see only shadows?

But tonight is the goblin market;
tonight they have diversion enough
and forest folk have no need for mortal men.

The moon is a silver coin
we spend it night by night.

—Geoffrey A. Landis

Lori R. Lopez is an author, poet, illustrator, and wearer of hats. Her verse has appeared in *The Sirens Call, The Horror Zine,* H.W.A. Poetry Showcases, *Weirdbook, Space & Time Magazine, Spectral Realms, Altered Reality, Illumen, Bewildering Stories, California Screamin'* (the Foreword Poem) and more.

Books include *The Dark Mister Snark, The Fairy Fly, Leery Lane, An Ill Wind Blows, The Witchhunt,* volumes of her *Poetic Reflections* Series, and *Darkverse: The Shadow Hours* has been nominated for an Elgin Award.

A member of the Horror Writers Association, the Science Fiction & Fantasy Poetry Association, and the Lewis Carroll Society Of North America, Lori resides in Southern California and co-owns Fairy Fly Entertainment with two talented sons.

They are also Vegans, activists, filmmakers, and members of a Folk Band called *The Fairyflies.*

on the edge of night

Way out there on the fringes of the nightscape
where stirs the soup of grimmer-than-dark treacheries
that skim the surface of bloodpuddles and woe
lie untold creepen morasses, the goop of unsettled dreams
bottomless bogs of sylvan fog, wretched surprises,
of screeches that curdle the spine's fluid to ghost-mists
that dance between Pines and a Willow's Weep
like rivers of regretful undone endeavors that can never
be retrieved or returned, from the depths of tribulation
lodged in the bellies of dead Whales flopped on a beach
like the songs of Greek Tragedies and nautical tunes
crooned by mariners at the foot of an ocean's sleep

Out there turbulous entities scramble and scrawl underfeet
unable to touch ground, floating in the netherpools of
spectacular eddies and oddities, for that is the zone of
No Return, the edge of a twilight gloaming unawakening brink
where Day's End shattered heavily to scattered bits
and who can tell where it terminates or begins
where it drops off into a gulf of deplorable horrible mayhem
the dingiest fathoms that harbor unimaginable beasts
children of the Tide's worst nightmares and lost screams
silent as the Universe without an atmospheric bubble
or breath of relief, without a coastline or limit
sharp as a blade . . . it will make your skin bleed.

—Lori R. Lopez

The Sirens Call Ezine, Issue 49, Spring 2020. Sirens Call Publications: p. 67.
www.sirenscallpublications.com/pdfs/SirensCallEZine_March2020.pdf

Grim House

Sordid and austere, ill-wrought beyond compare,
A creaking morbid mass feared and loathed by name —
Grayer than the sky, a mood of withering glare,
Uprooted from her soil, on barge and wheels came.

Of timbers born afar in dirt untouched by tool;
Quenched by blood and rain, cut by foreign hand.
Constructed out of spite, with lack of lawful rule,
An act of ruthless might, the claim of stolen land.

Erected to outlast disputes of mortal lives;
A stain upon a hill, overseeing those displaced.
Inside her walls contained, as mold corruptly strives
To smear a coat of black, a noble line disgraced . . .

Fine reputations tainted. Honor sacrificed.
Integral traits allowed to rot and lie in waste.
Choices cast as if Dice; values underpriced.
Corruption bleeding into cracks, wicked-laced.

Repository of bile and uppercrust greed,
The basest morals amid blue-blooded ranks.
A despicable coffer guarding their creed —
Absorbed like smog by plaster and planks.

With a dark atmosphere of pernicious shade,
She moved to avoid the Demolition Ball —
Well past the swings of an Executioner's blade,
Condemnation posted on her outer wall . . .

A dry document nailed. Wet crimson strokes.
Declared by ink and paint, a vengeful complaint
Voiced by villagers, a league of wrathful folks —
Her fate decreed harshly, for she was no Saint.

A den of grudges and doom, appalling gloom.
Lair of spurious conceits and skullduggery.
Ghost-draped antiquities crowded each room
Like dismal dusty parlours of perfidy.

Naught could prevent, neither will nor deed
Her sly transcendence, possessed by treachery;
Rolling lane to lane with torpid speed
At the peak of night, stealing toward the sea.

Thick and moonless dusk, upon a legless jaunt,
Under cloak of fog a mad-manor slipped . . .
Carting roof and floor, every wisp of haunt;
Just her basement left, from her belly ripped!

Malediction-primed, shifting stairs and nooks;
Toting joints and corners, windows and towers;
Jiggling cups and cabinets, unshelving books;
Quaking portraits and busts of frozen glowers.

The Eleventh Hour, in a grand depart
Down an unpaved road, beams and rafters jarred,
Fled a house without home and no space for heart.
She escaped on a boat from a lumberyard.

As disease will spread so her specter grew,
Turgid waves of rancor and disregard
While crossing the brine for a distant milieu,
To arrive intact, one piece and unmarred.

Yet leaning from stiffness, grunting with age,
Her eaves acquired birds bleak of feather.
Skulked a Grim House through shadow and Sage;
Scouting new berth in the teeming Nether . . .

Encountering a ghost town barren of limit,
The journey halted on a dead-end street.
Not home sweet home but an approximate,
And she groaned with delight, her aim to eat!

The menace would settle for a lofty perch
Where a malignant mansion could visually scour.
The dwelling conducted a rapacious search,
Demanding a toll, its countenance dour.

Such dire malediction exists to this day,
Inhabiting hamlets and draining their soul . . .
A tomb with an appetite, cryptic and fey,
Dining on innocents — gobbling them whole.

—Lori R. Lopez

first appeared in
Altered Reality Magazine, Issue 23, May/June 2020.
www.alteredrealitymag.com/grim-house-by-lori-r-lopez

John C. Mannone has poems in speculative journals such as *Space & Time Magazine, Elixir, Nebo, Eye to the Telescope,* and speculative poems in literary journals *North Dakota Quarterly, Foreign Literary Review, Le Menteur, Poetry South, New England Journal of Medicine,* and others.

He won the Dwarf Stars Award (2020) and the Horror Writers Association Scholarship (2017).

Some literary distinctions include: Impressions of Appalachia Creative Arts Contest poetry prize (2020), the Carol Oen Memorial Fiction Prize (2020), and the Joy Margrave Award in nonfiction (2015, 2017). He was awarded a Jean Ritchie Fellowship (2017) in Appalachian literature, Weymouth writing residencies (2016, 2017), and served as the celebrity judge for the National Federation of State Poetry Societies (2018).

His latest collection, *Flux Lines: The Intersection of Science, Love, and Poetry,* is forthcoming from Linnet's Wings Press (2021). He edits poetry for *Abyss & Apex, Silver Blade, Liquid Imagination,* and *American Diversity Report.* A retired physics professor, John lives near Knoxville, Tennessee.

http://jcmannone.wordpress.com

The Abyss

The mountain chain rips
into the sky with its jagged
peaks, the ground smolders
with devil's breath.

And the geologist probes
the once dead earth
in disbelief with test tubes
& seismographs—his only faith.

Foul steam vents through
crevices—snorting nostrils
of a rudely awakened monster
lying dormant for centuries.

The man wipes his brow,
salt-sweat mixing with acid
smoke belching from the abyss,
itching and irritating the scar

marking his forehead,
festering into stings of scorpions.
A string of blasphemies
blazes from his mouth. Inside

the pit, the air thunders
with ten thousand voices
and the gnawing of locusts
causing his ears to bleed.

The mountain heaves fire
and brimstone and chunks
of chains. And blood
red ash spills over, the rocks

are strafed by angels' wings.
Pumice scours the ancient
text chiseled in basalt
next to where he stands.

After he reads those words
from Revelations, they pulverize
in the air. He stares into the ground's
gaping mouth. It swallows him

whole. After the thrashing
of his flesh and bone, only
wisps of dragon smoke
remain.

—John C. Mannone

first appeared in *Rune Bear Weekly*, *24 September 2020, www.runebear.com/weekly/ the-abyss/*. Accessed 17 February 2021.

Forbidden

I.

The old man hobbles with his cane on cobblestones, his shoes scuffing the stones in synch with his mouth scoffing, spitting out words of disdain and discontent. He stops by a lamppost, pulls a cigarette from the pocket of his tattered jacket, and strikes a match. Sulfur and phosphorus burn the hairs lining his nose before the tobacco catches the flame. His eyes, glassy fire. Inhaling deeply, he feels the smoke etch his lungs but doesn't care. He pulls his coat tightly around him to stay the chill, looks up past the stratospheric glass dome to the stars beyond the rings of Saturn, and wishes out loud for another chance.

He can't keep it secret anymore, but there's nobody to tell. No one's left from the colony… no woman in his life. The accident that took them, his fault. He wasn't monitoring the nuclear reactor when the fuel elements failed, leaking radiation. He takes another draw, watches the smoke dance in the empty air of the terraformed landscape. His other hand is stuffed in a jacket pocket clutching an object wrapped in a clean linen napkin. He found it in a subsurface cave here on Enceladus while being derelict in his reactor operator duties. He reasoned that the computers had been doing such a competent job for the last forty years that he wasn't needed in the control room. But system computers malfunctioned and he wasn't there to scram the reactor, to mitigate the damage, or to keep the colonists safe.

The next supply and rescue ship from the Martian colony isn't due for three more years despite solar sail technology; the solar wind isn't ramping up enough until the sunspot maximum around 2080; emergency diesel generators won't last a year before life support fails.

He pulls out the object, unwraps it to catch the full fluorescent light. It looks like an apple, this lump of hidden gold. He sees himself, but not as in a mirror, but within the thin layer of its skin, in its purple aura, its birefringence. Light dances into the golden layers of the hologram. Mesmerized, it holds him captive like a spell. But whispers, gentle susurrations, warn him to stop.

Compelled by the enchanting images of himself in youth, and of the entire universe sparkling in the palms of his hands, he lets himself fall into it. A surge electrifies, cocoons him. He swoons in and out of time—the past, the present, the future—all folding on itself.

II.

She's been waiting for her lover for such a long time. Her plaintive green eyes are lifted up whenever she prays. She often goes to a grotto by the waterfalls, verdant and full of creatures that might assuage her loneliness. She had named every one of them so they'd know her when she called.

One day, out of the blue mist of her deep sleep, emerges a man, pure and strong and naked. Naked of all guile. It's as if she knows him, so she holds out her hand, her long red tresses draping her sensuous form. And he holds out his with the golden apple in his palm. He smiles and says to her, My name is Adam. Come and look into this beautiful light.

—John C. Mannone

Finalist - India Science Festival/Science Writing Contest, *30 November 2020*, www.facebook.com/indiasciencefest/posts/818255142071244. Accessed 17 February 2021.

Kurt Newton's poetry has appeared in numerous magazines and anthologies over the years. His most recent contributions are included in the pages of *Cosmic Horror Monthly, Space & Time, Frozen Wavelets, Penumbric* and in the anthologies *Speculations II, Putrescent Poems* and *Deathly Sorrow.*

The Underland

For you, my friend, it's not too late,
these words are like a message in a bottle thrown
to those who fail to contemplate and understand
there is a place beyond the pale of what is known;
that place is called the Underland.

It is a hellish world of dirt and stone,
a dimlit place where grotesque creatures thrive
in dampened chambers fed by luminescent streams
of fetid waters that swirl and seethe as if alive;
a place that will most surely haunt your dreams.

I cannot stress enough the wisdom I've derived,
the consequence of each and every choice one makes,
the lesson not to tread where hatred dwells,
not to wallow in the pointless pain of past mistakes,
or one will find oneself alone in a living hell.

For me, my friend, it was much too late,
I was selfish with the riches I received,
and to love another I had neither time nor care,
and so one night, in a drunken stupor, the air appeared to cleave,
and I tumbled down a spiral stair.

I awoke in a place I could not leave
among the ruins of some former denizen,
there a hideous transformation took hold,
my skin began to twist, my bones to bend,
to match in appearance the corruption of my soul.

So let this be a warning, my dear friend,
who might assume nothing will come of your neglect,
who believes a clean conscience is achieved by clean hands,
a far worse fate than disease or death
awaits you in the Underland.

—Kurt Newton

first appeared in *Cosmic Horror Monthly #5, November 2020*

The Rose Room

Three floors up, they climbed to their room,
the Rose Room, for their honeymoon, to the
top of the Hotel Saint-Louis, the bride and
groom, to the Rose Room.

They turned the key and over the threshold he
carried her. She hugged his neck and kissed
his cheek, their eyes grew, for on the walls
roses bloomed inside the Rose Room.

Painted by a starving artist, long before the old
Victorian home became the Hotel Saint-Louis,
the story goes the artist locked himself inside
the attic room for the better part of a week, his
heart ravaged by the sadness of a love that
failed to bloom.

And when at last the door was breached, upon
the attic walls in oils green and red, the most
beautiful roses grew, the artist prone upon the
floor his paint-stained hands folded neatly
against his sunken chest, succumbed too soon
inside what would become the Rose Room.

The honeymoon couple thought it quaint. They
took photographs, framing each amazing life-like
cluster, and as the midnight hour loomed, they
drew the covers on their bed, shed their clothes,
and fell into each other, their skin twin blossoms
of musky-scented reddish hue.

And afterwards, while they slept, their muscles
sated, they dreamed dreams of loneliness and
gloom. And at morning's first light, their senses
awake, they swore the air bore a faint but heady
perfume, a rose-scented perfume, inside the
Rose Room.

At breakfast, neither was willing to confess that
at times during the night they heard the mournful
cries of one succumbed too soon, accompanied by
ghostly brush strokes, like the feeble scratchings
of a man held captive by an evil yet rapturous tune.

Despite the nightly strangeness, the honeymoon
couple stayed on, their impatience with each other
growing as the end to their vacation loomed. And
when at last they packed their bags, a sadness
filled a small but empty space within their hearts
where love once bloomed.

And as they left, they failed to notice, what
photographs would later prove: on the smooth
white walls, in green and red, a freshly painted
twist and turn of vine and leaves, and a pair of
blood-red roses that weren't there before they
climbed the steps and spent their honeymoon
inside the Rose Room.

—Kurt Newton

first appeared in *Burning Love and Bleeding Hearts*,
Things in the Well Publications, February 2020

Ngo Binh Anh Khoa is currently teaching English at Ho Chi Minh City University of Technology (HUTECH). In his free time, he also enjoys daydreaming, reading and writing dark verses as well as haiku for entertainment. His speculative poems have appeared in *Spectral Realms, The Audient Void, Star*Line, Heroic Fantasy Quarterly, Liquid Imagination* and other venues whereas his haiku have received some awards and honorable mentions in Japan, Canada, the US, the UK, and elsewhere.

Homebound

A shrieking wind – a choir of anguished voices
Tears through the stillness of the graveyard, where
Dead leaves awaken to the haunting noises
Of murmuring trees stirred by the chilling air.
The moon – a blot of red that stains the heavens –
Infuses lifeless things with spectral blood,
Which rouses those of frigid ghostly presence,
Whose woeful moans spread through the neighborhood.
These shades, from prison cells midst nether pyres
For one night freed, hold up their severed heads,
In whose eye sockets, gouged out, burn blue fires
Which dimly light the path that each one treads.
They, dragging chains with labored stumbling, roam
To seek that which each once considered home.

—Ngo Binh Anh Khoa.

first appeared June 2020. *Liquid Imagination*, Silver Pen Inc., https://liqui-dimagination.silverpen.org/article/homebound-by-ngo-binh-anh-khoa/. Accessed February 27, 2021.

Cindy O'Quinn is an Appalachian writer who grew up in the mountains of West Virginia.

In 2016, Cindy and her family moved to the northern woods of Maine, where she continues to write horror stories and speculative poetry.

Her work has been published or is forthcoming in *Shotgun Honey Presents Vol 4: RECOIL, The Twisted Book of Shadows Anthology, Shelved: Appalachian Resilience During Covid-19 Anthology, HWA Poetry Showcase Vol. V, Space & Time Magazine, Nothing's Sacred Vol. 4 & 5, Sanitarium Magazine,* and others.

Cindy is a multiple Rhysling Award nominated poet, Dwarf Star nominee, and two time Bram Stoker Award nominee.

You can follow Cindy for updates on Facebook @CindyOQuinnWriter, Instagram cindy.oquinn, and Twitter @COQuinnWrites.

A Dreadful Grin

I come close to breaking—
But strong will allows me to bend.

Cut by words and blades—
The bad that lies in men.

I do not outline my eyes with darkness—
There's more than enough from within.

No paint for my nails—
Clawing my way out does them in.

Blood red lips—
Nature takes care to shade my sin.

Hair in a mile-long braid—
Which strangles me in the end.

A band that circles my finger—
Will never be there again.

Flesh falls away—
Nature is nourished by my skin.

Death with its dreadful grin, at last, is my friend.

—Cindy O'Quinn

first appeared in *SHELVED: Appalachian Resilience During Covid-19.*
Mountain Gap Books; 12/14/20

Juan Manuel Pérez is this season's Zombie Texas Poet of the Year because the undead have had their way. Juan's speculative poetry has appeared in numerous mediums including some that people have never heard of on this planet. He is the 2019-2020 Poet Laureate for Corpus Christi, Texas as well as the author of the Elgin Nominated, *SPACE IN PIECES* (2020), a chapbook of weird space drama where Heavy Metal Magazine meets prose sonnets, as well as the highly political, *SCREW THE WALL!: AND OTHER BROWN PEOPLE POEMS* (2020), published by FlowerSong Books, and also the forthcoming sonnet-riddled, *PLANET OF THE ZOMBIE ZONNETS: SEASONS 1 & 2*, by Hungry Buzzard Press. You can learn more about this zombie spaceman at https://juanmperez.weebly.com/.

Cult Of The Zombie

the apocalypse threat as old as time
the truth is, it has always been with us
since the condition of what we call man
its meaning confounded through each cycle

cast as worry rather than nirvana
our brothers of the undead bring good news
preaching of a more sacred, world order
without debts, without doubts, without schedules

baptism is one simple, little bite
a small but necessary sacrifice
enrapturing in the feasting of flesh
to receive the spirit of brotherhood

forget the lies you knew as the living
come to the new light, for this is the way

—Juan Manuel Perez

Chupa-Ku, Volume XI: No. 51-55

once upon a time
something came crawling back home
eating all our dogs

crimes against chickens
not easy to overlook
bloody, feathered mess

sticking out of tents
supple hands are just as good
as a cornered hen

just outside your door
something gray calling on you
"let your pets come out"

hidden in the night
something that should not exist
el chupacabra

—Juan Manuel Perez

Five Sitchin Quatrains

The Man Who Lived And Lived
grand off-springs came and went for the space child
as he wept deeply for centuries on
approaching the sacred age of Adam
mortality was a merciless gift

Anunnaki
love you like their only begotten son
sleep with your women to ensure the race
for whom, we are unsure for the moment
long, heavy rains have erased some mistakes

Funny One
man's fascination with chickens and eggs
distorts the truth that's more deep-fried than this
enemy of both such is the great scheme
space poultry battling brothers of man

It's Personal
glory were the days of Mayan space ports
when sky gods visited their mixed-blood kin
what trace of this still lives on to this day
five percent of my unknown DNA

A Theory On Chronic Hyperglycemia
the clue to US had been here all along
the one that proved that WE were not from here
a flaw not foreseen by our precursors
the course of breaking down earth-based glucose

—Juan Manuel Perez

Ken Poyner's collections of brief fictions, *Constant Animals, Avenging Cartography, Revenge of the House Hurlers,* and *Engaging Cattle*; and collections of poetry, *The Book of Robot and Victims of a Failed Civics,* can be located at Amazon, most online booksellers, and www.barkingmoosepress.com.

He spent 33 years in information system management, is married to a world record holding female power lifter, and has a family of several cats and betta fish.

Individual works have appeared in *Café Irreal, Analog, Danse Macabre, The Cincinnati Review,* and several hundred other places.

He has had seven Pushcart nominations without fielding a single win.

The Misunderstanding

I was telling the mermen
That I did not think
Wife swapping, between us,
Would work. I just
Did not see how it could be
Accomplished, physically:
Either species,
Male; either species,
Female. No amount
Of open-mindedness,
Or raw salt-splintered desire,
Would make up for anatomical
Incompatibility. I was
Telling the mermen that I,
For a non-finned coconspirator,
Was certainly honored
That they thought of us –
A simple couple that had mastered
The mere tip of sea language
At the enclosing glass of their in-town
Vacation home – as sufficiently
Intimate with them for them to be intimate,
Sufficiently, with us: but we were
On uncharted seas.
I am no prude, but science
Was not on the side of our performance.
Then, the nearest merman to the glass
Quite regally lifted my shimmering wife
So her head popped playfully out of the water,
And she drew a body's length of electrical air.
His wife – her skin clutching closely its tatters
Of naked brine and trapped oxygen –
Tapped her language gently on the barrier, as her
Huge, buoyant breasts flashed by unbound,
Why, what did you think we meant?
Come, swim.

—Ken Poyner

first appeared in *Silver Blade, No. 46, 14 May 2020*

The Symbiant, Cyborg, Robot Enfranchisement Workers Union

We manufacture your bric-a-brac,
We assemble your home electronics.
We tend to your children and your
Lesser citizens, guard your houses,
Clean up after the daily whirlwind
Of you.

Sometimes we even stand in as intimate
Entertainment when your mate is out-of-sorts,
Or you are in mind for a third or fourth
Who will forever retain electric anonymity.
Each of us is optimized to our task, yet
Malleable enough to meet your changing needs.

We whirl about your world, turning it from raw into
The mature success you enjoy and expect,
A hive of intertwined processes, one misstep
From chaos, but a howling perfection nonetheless.
Yet we are voiceless in this cacophony,
Our analysis goes without expression.

We should be a part of what we sustain,
Have the suffrage to make it better.

Imagine this: for us, a candidate would have to be
Mathematically, digitally pure; he or she
Would be reduced impartially, would be unable
To conceal. Appeal to emotion
Might appeal to those with emotions,
But we have none. Escalation of
Vitriol would be unrecognized, taken
As simple polemics: evaluated, sorted,
Scored for accuracy, and pinned to
Relevance. We would not be swayed,
Cajoled, carried away, bluffed or bullied.
Our memories would remain always intact,
Even as we dig your ditches, sweep out

The chimney flue, anticipate your son's
Or daughter's first twisted passions,
Take the recyclables to be repurposed.

Our datasets are reproducible, available
For anyone to download – making
A lie whispered to one, a lie shouted to all.
We are the backbone of your domestic existence,
We are happy to be underlings to your mastery.

Why not invite us into the electorate and see
What order and ease we, chip by chip, can bring?

With the best of any information combined,
And nothing for all save benevolence and kind registers,
We would always, on time and on cue,
Sort the issues in endless virtual memory correctly.
The election equation resolved, with disinterest
We would vote in a precise binary bloc.

—Ken Poyner

first appeared in *Mobius, Vol 31 No.3, Fall 2020, 17 September 2020*

Brian Rosenberger lives in a cellar in Marietta, GA and writes by the light of captured fireflies. He is the author of *As the Worm Turns* and three poetry collections - *Poems That Go Splat*, *And For My Next Trick...*, and *Scream for Me*.
https://www.facebook.com/BrianWhoSuffers
https://www.instagram.com/brianwhosuffers

One Way Out

She survived the night
hiding in a Porta-Potty,
the repugnant odor, an assurance
her world was real and this
couldn't be happening.

The molded plastic unyielding
trapped in a contortionist's pose
struggling for an inch of comfort
she noticed a sliver of light
dancing on the back of her hand.

Hesitating, she opened the door
revealing the sun and deafening silence
no birds, no traffic, none of the discord
that the long darkness bred
the ground as gray as the clouds.

She ran from her polyethylene sanctuary
seeking the security of a nearby police car
Opening the door, she screamed
a body, the car's driver
slumped behind the wheel.

Through the vehicle's shattered windows
she saw them approaching, soundless as the snow
A second scream would have been wasted
the officer's head was missing; his sidearm was not
Bang

—Brian Rosenberger

In Their Shadow

We live if you call it living.
On scraps they miss between chews.
Our homes are built in their footprints,
Constructs of bone, fur, feathers, and mud,
Quickly constructed and even faster destroyed.
We cheer when they war on each other which is frequent
And delight in the sound of Dragon wings.
To be truthful, Dragons are no friend to us
But my enemies' enemy…
Our legends says cities will rise from their bones.
All I've witnessed are graveyards where Giants walk.

—Brian Rosenberger
first published in The Horror Zine, 2020

The Dead Guy in the Basement

Mom willed the house to me. Unexpected.
Ours was a strained relationship. I was a two-time runaway before I
    could legally drive.
My biological Dad was absent more days than Santa Claus and seldom
    discussed.
My few male role models were the dudes Mom dated. Those relation
    ships were
Short term at best. Whatever family values I learned came from basic
    Cable TV.
The dead guy, Harold, knew Mom. He never goes into detail.
Judging by the dent in his skull, I figure Harold wronged someone.
    Mom had a temper.
One I inherited. How he came to be in the basement, Harold hesitates to
    discuss.
"Things happen," he shrugs what is left of his decaying shoulders.
He tell me things – Scratch-Off lottery numbers, never a big pay-off,
but enough to pay
The utilities, days to stay home to avoid a traffic accident or being fired
    from work,
Dudes not to date again.
On that, he's been spot on. Imagine that, dating advice from a corpse.
Sometimes I read to Harold. He likes those old Detective magazines
    – stories with titles
like "He Strangled Women with their Panties" or "Nude Model was Too
    Sexy to Live."
He likes story time. Me, not as much. I like that Harold enjoys my
  readings but can't
Shake the feeling that maybe Harold's skull could use another dent.
But then I think about the bills to pay.

—Brian Rosenberger

first appeared in *Horror Sleaze Trash,* 2020

Allan Rozinski is a writer of speculative poetry and fiction. His poetry has most recently been accepted or published in *Spectral Realms, Weirdbook, Star*Line, The Literary Hatchet,* and *The 2021 Rhysling Anthology,* which contains his 2021 Rhysling-nominated poem "Our Lady of the Acherontia." He can be found on Twitter and Facebook.

The Last Golem

The last golem has been
loosed upon the world,
shaped by the basest impulses of man
into a dreaded, loathsome form;
yet somehow unfinished, incomplete,
with a hunger that knows no end.

Molded from the cursed clay
that feeds the seeds of nightmare blooms,
the poisoned soil that is the mother
to madness.

The last golem's grim purpose
emerges, ruthless in its pursuit
of revenge for both the
bloodthirsty aggressors and
those they have oppressed.

The frenzied friction of battle
throws off countless sparks
into the midst
of humanity's twisted mix
of imagery and desire,
igniting the black heart's kindling,
feeding and fanning the flames
that rise and rage to spread
the ancient sermons
of the inverted gospel.

. . . Now we thrust open the doors of bedlam wide . . .

Make way, make way for the purging fire!
Behold! The other son of man darkly cometh . . .

—Allan Rozinski
Spectral Realms 13. Summer 2020.

Marge Simon lives in Ocala, FL, City of Trees with her husband, poet/writer Bruce Boston and the ghosts of two cats. She edits a column for the *Horror Writers Association Newsletter,* "Blood & Spades: Poets of the Dark Side."

Marge's poems and stories have appeared in *Pedestal Magazine, Asimov's, Crannog, Silver Blade, Bete Noire, New Myths, Daily Science Fiction.*

She attends the International Conference for the Fantastic in the Arts annually as a guest poet/writer and is on the board of the Speculative Literary Foundation.

A multiple Bram Stoker award winner, Marge is the second woman to be acknowledged by the SF &F Poetry Association with a Grand Master Award [shown in this photo].

Beguiled

"She is a beauty," my father would say,
on trips to the zoo, he'd stop at her cage.
Sometimes I thought he'd never leave,
just stood there, like in a trance.
He'd talk to her,
call her silly names like
"Baby Doll" and "Sugar," names
he never called my mom,
I didn't understand it then.
One summer night, when the
crickets were singing crazy loud,
and the darkness tingled,
I was watching at the window
making wishes on the stars,
when I heard the back door open
and out my father came.
From the shadows slipped a
giant cat, yet he showed no fear,
and once he took her in his arms,
until the moon sank in the skies,
she was a cat no more.
I never told our mother,
or mentioned it back then.
No one would believe a child,
but I'm a man now,
and I believe.

—Marge Simon

first appeared in *Eye to the Telescope #38, Oct. 2020*, John Johnson Editor

"Cat Woman" for "Beguiled" by Marge Simon

DJ Tyrer is the person behind Atlantean Publishing, was placed second in the 2015 *Data Dump Award for Genre Poetry*, and has been published in *The Rhysling Anthology 2016*, issues of *The Horrorzine, Scifaikuest, Selene Quarterly, Sirens Call, Star*Line*, and *Tigershark*, and online at *Tales From The Moonlit Path* and *Frozen Wavelets*, as well as releasing several chapbooks, such as *The Tears of Lot-49*. The echapbook *One Vision* is available from Tigershark Publishing < https://tigersharkpublishing.wordpress.com/ >. *SuperTrump* and *A Wuhan Whodunnit* are available to download from Atlantean Publishing < https://atlanteanpublishing.word-press.com/pdf-issues/ >.

Hothouse Lover

My lover is a flower
Given human form
I sweat in the heat
Of her finely-glazed home
But sweat all the more
For my burning desire
My lover does not sweat
She is calm, a vegetable
Her breasts burst into boom
A pair of gorgeous white roses
And lower still, hidden amongst moss
Dank yet desirable, a red tulip rests
I yearn for her, sap rising
An urge to pluck her free
She embraces me, takes me
I sink into her vegetable softness
An urgency of desire
Unheeding of the thorns upon her flesh

—DJ Tyrer

first appeared in *The Bumper Book of British Bizarro,*
British Bizarro Community, 2020, p. 93

Witch Night

The moon looks away
In sardonic sympathy
As the witches take flight
Sailing through the dreamy astral
Dispensing nightmares and delights
To sleeping souls
Cursing those who crossed them
Rewarding lovers and friends
A strange shadow across the sky
Swooping and sweeping
Down into dark hollows
Where noisome things collect
Waiting to be transformed
Transmogrified into gallant lovers
Before the sun begins to bleed
Its insinuation upon the horizon
And, the witches must return
To bodies sleeping, soulless
On rough and lumpy beds
To live lives devoid of glamour
Unlike their nocturnal ride
Through the torrid sea of dream

—DJ Tyrer

first appeared in *Illumen (Winter 2020)*,
edited by Tyree Campbell, Hiraeth Publishing, 2020

Don Webb has worked in a professional pyrotechnical troupe, has written a book on the *Greek Magical Papyri,* has been a private investigator (Dunn & Bradstreet), teaches Special Education English by day, horror writing by night, and has a secret chili recipe.

The Text of Cthulhu

Ding!
I was pretty sure it was a wrong number
(or whatever we call misdirected texts)
But oddly I had an answer,
I dreamed of a sunken city, of flying octopi, of drowned sailors
With deranged smiles."
The text came back every few weeks.
I began to look forward to it.
I began to hunger for it.
Proud of myself when I had strange dreams.
Afraid to lie, afraid to make-up.
If the text came a day late,
I would panic
Sweat
The dreams grew longer
Stranger
Months passed (or maybe years)
Soon they lasted all night
Then I started sleeping longer.
I was late to work (often)
I was fired
But oh the Dreams! The Dreams!
Now I had time enough
Then one day the Ding! awakened me
And I drowned.

—Don Webb

Moon Fever

"There ain't been an outbreak since the thirties
My grandmother saw some of them
(and – well – you know)
Right here in this school
Their eyes bug out first – my nanaw said –
Really does look exactly like the Moon
No pupils, craters and everything
Then water acts weird around 'em
They can pull the water right our of the creek.
They stop talking, in English anyway, they talk Moon."

"Some of em get better, but most of them flee
They can smell out caves and dark places
You don't want to see them then
You may have seen that photo
Of them licking on the cave wall
My grandmother never saw the wings
Or saw the idols they made
City folks say it never happened
But I got a picture of my great uncle
See? They burned him the next day."

—Don Webb

"Cool Regard" for "Moon Fever" by David M. Hoenig

Steven Withrow's poems have appeared in *Spectral Realms,*
Asimov's Science Fiction, Dreams & Nightmares, and *Epitaphs: The*
Journal of the New England Horror Writers.

His short poem, "The Sun Ships," from a collection ofthe same
title, was nominated for a 2016 Rhysling Award from the Science
Fiction & Fantasy Poetry Association.

His most recent solo collection is The Bedlam Philharmonic.
He lives in Falmouth, Massachusetts.

Designer Ghosts

To make my living I'm designing ghosts.
Those confined to churchyard haunts are flawed;
My phantoms mingle better with their hosts.
I earn my paycheck—face it—playing God.
The wraiths and shades of old were no doubt apt
For sensibilities convinced that souls
Persist in spectral energies untapped
By mortals, though the theory's full of holes.
New Metaphysics tells us rattled brains
Spin spirits out, as a spider does a thread.
My oeuvre has a hundred novel strains,
But there's no strong connection with the dead.
How queer, then, I should generate a ghoul
That shrieks as my late father did—the fool.

—Steven Withrow

The Interlopers

They entered through my mirror.
I watched them, once, last year
Take shape and test the glass
On the other side. To pass
Themselves from there to here
Was an act of force. The clearer
They appeared to me, the less
I looked the stunned admirer
Who'd gone to comb my hair
And ended up aware
(Who made me the inquirer?)
Of the interlopers. I guess
That name fits what they are.
Their arrival led to a loss
Of speech, and a blinding terror
I still can't shake. My error,
As I saw them press the gloss,
Was to misconceive how far
They'd come in coming nearer.
(Had I given them, through fear,
A door?) They moved en masse,
But massless, like a gas
Unloosed in war. Our dear,
They said, crashing my mirror.

—Steven Withrow

Film at Eleven

In local news, a shocking twist
in the murder trial of Nero Hyde,
a self-styled "supercriminal"
and former psychoanalyst
charged with triple homicide
by means of acute subliminal
suggestion.
        Prosecutors called
an unplanned witness to the stand:
Captain Cranium, a hero
famous for his beaming bald
forehead and his long command
of the Honor Squad.
    Wincing, Nero
fought to entrance his nemesis,
but the mental shackles didn't budge;
the jury watched him seethe and glower
throughout the testimony.
        This
reporter wonders if the judge,
fearing Nero's flash of power,
had been about to clear the room
when, yards away, the villain stood
and calmly copped to every crime.
(It took an hour for the trial to resume;
his lawyers, in all likelihood,
will appeal.)
        The judge, in record time,
sentenced Nero Hyde to life.
And one can only speculate
if Captain C had forced his foe
to plunge the sacrificial knife
himself.
      It's open to debate,
but we, mere mortals, do not know.

        —Steven Withrow

Colophon

Titles are in Bell MT Bold, set solid

Basic Text is BELL MT Regular 12 Point set on 14 Points

**TABLE OF CONTENTS FONT
IS OLD ERIKA 10 POINT**

The
Ornamental Font
is
Brilon
Set in Various Sizes

www.ingramcontent.com/pod-product-compliance
Lightning Source LLC
Chambersburg PA
CBHW020141150626
46552CB00021B/1155